MOUSE AND SPOON

RABBIT TEA

SIMON SPOTLIGHT
An imprint of Simon & Schuster Children's Publishing Division
1230 Avenue of the Americas, New York, New York 10020
For more than 100 years, Simon & Schuster has championed authors and the stories they create.
By respecting the copyright of an author's intellectual property, you enable Simon & Schuster and the author to continue publishing exceptional books for years to come. We thank you for supporting the author's copyright by purchasing an authorized edition of this book.
This Simon Spotlight edition August 2025
Text © 2025 by Cynthia Rylant · Illustrations © 2025 by Janna Mattia
All rights reserved, including the right of reproduction in whole or in part in any form.
SIMON SPOTLIGHT, READY-TO-READ, and colophon are registered trademarks of Simon & Schuster, LLC.
For information about special discounts for bulk purchases, please contact Simon & Schuster Special Sales at 1-866-506-1949 or business@simonandschuster.com.
Simon & Schuster strongly believes in freedom of expression and stands against censorship in all its forms.
For more information, visit BooksBelong.com.
The Simon & Schuster Speakers Bureau can bring authors to your live event. For more information or to book an event, contact the Simon & Schuster Speakers Bureau at 1-866-248-3049
or visit our website at www.simonspeakers.com.
Manufactured in the United States of America 0725 LAK
2 4 6 8 10 9 7 5 3 1
CIP data for this book is available from the Library of Congress.
ISBN 9781665962254 (hc)
ISBN 9781665962247 (pbk)
ISBN 9781665962261 (ebook)

MOUSE AND SPOON

RABBIT TEA

BY CYNTHIA RYLANT
ILLUSTRATED BY JANNA MATTIA

Ready-to-Read

Simon Spotlight
New York   Amsterdam/Antwerp   London
Toronto   Sydney/Melbourne   New Delhi

On Littleton Street
in a little town,
three little mice
had a bakery.

Tom was the youngest,

Ginger was the oldest,

and Piper was right in the middle.

Their shop was called
the Mouse and Spoon Bakery.
And it had large, bright windows.

Each morning
Tom shined them up.

All day long, someone was always
looking in the window.
Someone who was not even
thinking about iced buns
would start thinking about them.
That is how shop windows work.

So the mouse bakers put their prettiest cakes and cookies in the window.

Unless it was Bear Day.
Bears love Brown Bread.
So on Bear Day the windows
were full of that.

But all the other days were not about bears. And this day was about a rabbit.

The rabbit who went into
the Mouse and Spoon Bakery
seemed to be thinking
and thinking.

Then Ginger asked,
"May we help you?"
And the rabbit jumped
straight up into the air.

When the rabbit jumped,
Tom jumped.
Which made Piper jump.
Which made Ginger jump.
This is what happens
when a rabbit is around.

"I am having a tea for six mothers," said the rabbit, after everyone had landed. "Can you deliver Shortbread and Carrot Cakes?" she asked.

"Of course!" said Ginger.
"Rabbits do not like icing,"
added the rabbit.
Tom could not imagine
anyone not liking icing.
He was just about to say so
when Ginger put a paw
over his mouth.

"I will also need something for the children," said the rabbit on her way out.

"How many?" asked Ginger.

"Two hundred and sixteen," said the rabbit.

And she left.

That is the other thing about rabbits.
Really big families.

The three mouse bakers
went right to the kitchen.
They lined up the mixing bowls
and spoons and graters and pans.
"Let's bake!" said Ginger.
Ginger was Head Baker
and liked to get things rolling.

Shortbread was easy.
One part Sugar.
Two parts Butter.
Three parts Flour.

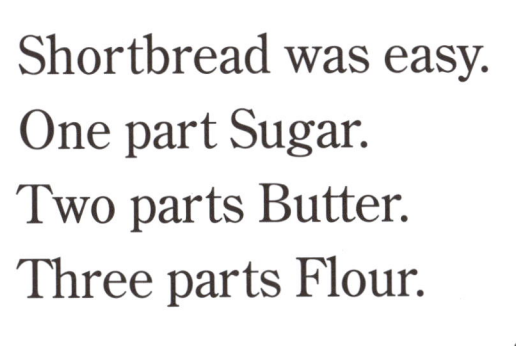

NO BAKING SODA! yelled Piper.
Piper always kept
everyone on their toes.

And when each Carrot Cake was pulled from the oven, Piper was in top form.
NO ICING FOR RABBITS! Piper yelled.

But when it was time to bake something for 216 rabbit children, none of the mice were on their mouse toes.
Not even Piper.

They were all flat on the floor.
Trying to come up with
something-times-216
easy to bake.

All three had to take a
little mouse nap first.
But when they woke up,
Ginger had it.
Cinnamon Sugar Sticks!
The mice baked long twisty
dough sticks for hours.

Then after stick Number 216,
they each had a wash
and went to bed.
Next day was tea.

The rabbit tea table
looked beautiful
when the mouse bakers arrived.
In the middle sat a swan
made of flowers.
The plates were pure china.
And every teapot had a cozy.

Even if rabbits are jumpy,
they make a lovely tea.

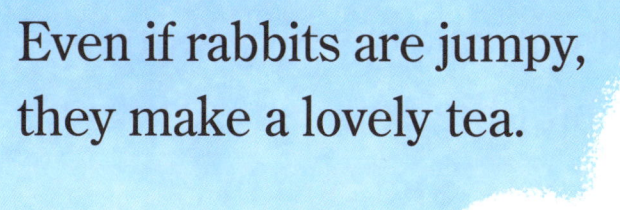

From the meadows all around, 216 rabbit children came running to the Mouse and Spoon Bakery truck.

The Cinnamon Sugar Sticks
did not even reach the tea table.
Off to the meadows they went.

The bakers were invited
to stay for the rabbit tea.
There was more than
enough to share.
And like most mothers,
the rabbits wanted
everyone well-fed.

But the little mice were tired and ready for a bit of quiet.

Tom took a few leaps
with the children
in the meadow.

Then the three bakers—
Ginger, Piper, and Tom—
returned to the Mouse and Spoon.
Where they brewed their own
little pot of tea.